BELDEN BOY

- the adventures of Peter McDugal

p.j. hartenaus

authorHOUSE®

AuthorHouse™
1663 Liberty Drive, Suite 200
Bloomington, IN 47403
www.authorhouse.com
Phone: 1-800-839-8640

First published by AuthorHouse   11/18/2008

ISBN: 978-1-4343-8351-8 (sc)

Library of Congress Control Number: 2008904602

Printed in the United States of America
Bloomington, Indiana

This book is printed on acid-free paper.

 Introduction

Long ago in the Northwest corner of Illinois, there was a little lead mining town called Galena. Located on a river, Galena was a bustling center of trade in the 1800s that had its share of ship captains, miners looking for lead, and a famous Civil War General who became our 18th President, Ulysses S. Grant. Even longer ago, hundreds of thousands of years ago, melting glaciers from our northern hemisphere pushed down across North America flattening the land in its path. The northwest corner of Illinois, Iowa, and Wisconsin, was left untouched, a driftless zone that was left unglaciated, leaving this area, to this day, incredibly beautiful. Hills, bluffs, valleys, and outcroppings of exposed rocks are the result and make this area unique. This territory is part of the Mississippi Valley.

Tucked away in the hills miles away from town, were families that lived and loved each other as they worked their farms. The children went to school, did their chores around the farm, and played by creeks and fields after their work was done. Children also had chores at school besides learning their lessons. The school in those days was a very important center for farm families. It was there that local people got together to hold meetings to decide on important things such as hiring teachers or purchasing goods for the school and the children. Sometimes they would elect people who would help to lead the farm community in a way that would benefit all.

This story is about a little boy who lived in the hills outside of Galena in the 1880s. He did some of the same things and had the same feelings about friendships as children do today. He may have lived long ago, but some things never change. So, pretend you are a living in those times and read about Peter McDugal, an eleven-year old boy, who attended Belden School, a one-room rock school house, in the hills of Galena's Territory.

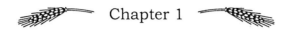

Chapter 1

Winter Morning

"Aw, Ma, do I have to go to school today? What with all that new snow last night, I might never make it over the hills! And anyway, Ma, I'm behind on my chores. Can't I stay home and get caught up? Please?" Ma doesn't answer right yet, but I know she's thinking 'bout what I said.

Ma just finished making my favorite buttermilk pancakes with sausage. The kitchen smells cozy, and I don't want to go. Looking out through the back door window at all that deep snow, I'm thinking that I could go sledding after my chores are done if Ma lets me stay home.

"Ma, I'm guessing that no one is going to school today. A person could get stuck out there real easy," I try asking Ma again, hoping she'll see it my way. Maybe our teacher was stuck in a snowdrift right now! Well, maybe.

"No, Peter. School is waiting for you. Go through the woods. Your Pa says there's less snow there," says Ma. Her voice tells me her mind is made up. There'll be no more talking 'bout it.

I grab my dinner pail and my leather strapped book and head out the back door. As I step on that 'ol creaky back step, I cover my eyes. It's blinding bright outside and colder than anything. The new snow covers the Galena hills like one of Ma's heavy quilts. I'm wishing I was still in bed under the quilt she made me last Christmas! Well, I'm guessing that I better head on out and make my way towards Belden School.

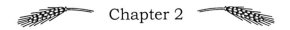

Chapter 2

BELDEN GREETING

Trudging through the snow, I can see that my boots barely make snow prints 'cause the deep crust is so frozen. I feel like I have potato sacks on my legs. I go up one hill and down the other. I'm wishing there weren't so many hills and valleys! My legs are getting so achy, and my fingers and toes feel as numb as my head did last summer when Franky hit me with a stick bat. I didn't see it coming, and I'm still not sure if he did it on purpose. Boy, I wish summer was here.

The only good thing 'bout walking to school today is that the snow is so high, I can step over the top wire of the fences. Sometimes I feel like a deer when it leaps over the drifts and fences real 'easy-like' with its white tail standing straight up like a flag.

As I come down the hill, I'm hoping that no smoke will be rising from Belden School's chimney. I'm thinking that if Miss Bishop didn't make it through the snow this morning, then maybe I can stop at the Kleck farm and visit the twins. I know their Pa would let me stay for a spell and warm up.

But jeepers, I can smell the burning oak coming from the chimney long before I set my eyes on it. I guess Miss Bishop didn't get stuck after all! She's not the only one who's waiting. I know that Belden School is waiting for me too...like it's alive or something. It's telling me to quit wasting time and get inside 'cause there are chores to do. I have to fetch wood for the stove and crack the ice so I can fill the bucket with water from the spring. If I don't have chores at home, I've got chores at school. It just ain't fair that I'm one of the oldest! Well, least ways it's warm inside.

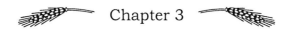

Chapter 3

TEACHER

"Good morning, Peter! Come on in. You're the only one who made it all the way to school. The others probably couldn't make it through the deep snow. They probably stayed home to help feed the animals. It must have been so hard for you to get through those drifts this morning. I'm amazed you even tried!" Miss Bishop says full of energy.

Miss Bishop is pretty and has brown curls, but that doesn't stop her from playing stickball with us outside during recess. She came to teach at Belden School at the beginning of our last harvest. I hear that her family lives up around Wisconsin way.

I look around but don't see the Kleck twins or Franky or any of my pals. I'm feeling mighty alone without the others, and my mind gets to wondering if I'll have to do their school lessons along with mine. I'm wishing real hard that I had stayed home!

But it looks like Miss Bishop might have different plans for me. "Peter, come and sit by the stove and let's chat for a spell," she says as she opens the door to the stove and puts in some of that dry old oak that Mr. Olson chopped for school last fall. It makes a crackling sound when it hits the fire, and it feels good to be warm again.

I'm surprised when she sits down and puts her feet up, boots and all, on the stove. I try it too, but have to move closer. My legs are too short. Then Miss Bishop talks on and on 'bout the snow and how she got to school that morning.

"Mr. Potts brought me over on the sleigh early this morning," she tells me. "The horses could barely get through. The wind was so cold that it stung our faces, but the snow is beautiful, isn't it Peter?"

I just nod.

As she is talking, I'm remembering that Miss Bishop is living with the Potts family this month. I'm feeling real sorry for Emily Potts. Seeing the teacher all day at school and then having to eat supper with her too, would be too much for me to take. I heard Ma and Pa say that schools like ours have to be built with lots of families around, so that the teacher can stay with different folks during the school year. The more I think 'bout that, the more I get scared. I know that my turn is coming up, and Miss Bishop will be living with me real soon.

"Poor Emily has the croup. She was coughing all night. Her Ma and Pa thought it best for her to stay in bed today. I think that was wise," Miss Bishop says as she stokes the fire. "Peter, how are things between you and Franky these days?"

I know why she's asking me that. Franky and I are having a hard time being friends lately. Franky's younger than me, but he's mighty big. His Ma and Pa's farm is over the hill from our farm. We only play together at recess. But lately, whenever we play games after lunch, he tries to steal my friends and get them on his side. Sometimes it works. Sometimes it don't. I don't know why he has to push everyone around including me, but when he does that, my stomach knots up inside. I guess we just kind of rub each other the wrong way. When recess comes around, I know it's not going to be fun, but I can't tell Miss Bishop that. Nope, this is something I just have to fix on my own. Things at school don't always work smoothly like a greased wheel.

So, I say, "Oh, its fine, Miss Bishop. Nothin' I can't handle."

She's speaking 'bout other things now, but I can tell this ain't the end of our talk 'bout Franky. Miss Bishop is always trying

11

to make things better in our school day for us. Sometimes she let's us play by the creek longer if it's a fine day out, or picnic by the old oak tree. I think Miss Bishop likes teaching at Belden School. Yep, like spring frogs jumping in the creek, I can count on hearing 'bout this again.

Miss Bishop keeps right on talking 'bout the cream-colored baby calf over at the Potts farm, and the vegetables she wants to plant in back of the school this spring, and what she was planning for us today. When she says "plans", though, I get to worrying again. Is she talking 'bout lessons?

"Peter, why don't you finish warming up and head on home? I'm sure there are plenty of chores for you to do, and I don't think any of the children will come by today. Do you think that would be fine?"

"Would it ever! I mean, yes, Miss Bishop, ma'm. I have plenty of chores to do at home. Th...thank you, Miss Bishop," I say, stumbling over my words and stumbling out the door at the same time. I'm also thinking I can head over to visit with the twins and maybe go home the long way by the frozen creek. By then, Ma should be making Pa a hot lunch, and I can walk right in, sit down, and...

"Go directly home, Peter," Miss Bishop stops my day dreaming in its tracks. How'd she know what I was thinking? But, as I walk out the door into the blinding snow again, she looks at me and winks, "and don't forget to go sledding after your chores are done. Have a good day!"

I climb out of the valley and up over the hill with those potato sack legs of mine. Then I turn to look back at my schoolhouse. Belden School, with it's smoke coming out of the chimney and the dry oak stacked on its side, seems to be winking at me, too, saying, "I'll be here tomorrow, Peter...waiting for you!"

Chapter 4

A Busy Spring

I like spring the best 'cause of all the sweet smells in the air. It feels like every season has a different smell, but spring is sweet. Pa says the spring rains splash the hills to wake them up after the winter....like washing your face after a long night's sleep.

Spring is a busy time on our farm. Everything is fresh and new. I help Pa and Ma harrow the fields back and forth to make the soil smooth. The soil smells so good after turning it up and planting that I could almost eat it. Pa's horses get excited, too. They toss their heads as they pull the plow through the fields. I use the hoe and make furrows ready to sow the seed. They need me to help get the soybeans, corn, potato plants and peas in the ground. We sow the grains in the field so that we will have food for us and our animals come winter. I know it's a long way off, but we've got to think 'bout the season coming up.

The birds are making their nests with anything they can find in the fields. I even saw a baby fawn the other day peeking at me through the woods. All the plants and animals seem happy now that spring is here.

There are things that I want to do, now that it's spring! I want to cross that creek over by Belden School. It's running high and fast from the melted winter snows, but I bet there are lots of frogs over there to catch. I want to also visit the Kleck farm 'cause they always have baby spring calves in their barn. I can't wait 'till I have my own someday.

Spring is fun in Galena's hills except for the rattlers. We have to wear tall boots when we're walking to school 'cause the rattlesnakes come out of the hills to lay on the rocks and get warm in the sun. They slither in the tall prairie grasses sneaky-like and sometimes I don't see them. One day, Maggie Brody forgot and left her boots on her back porch. She got bit walking to Belden School and hobbled all the way crying so loud that Miss Bishop thought she got attacked by Indians or something. Lucky for her it wasn't the poisonous kind.

"You've got to wear those boots!" Miss Bishop said to Maggie after she quieted down. Miss Bishop wears boots, too.

Yep, spring is sure busy. Belden School is busy too! Ma and Pa went to a meeting at school the other night. The town folks were making decisions on things I really don't understand. They were talking 'bout levying taxes, and voting for new people to run the school. I think they call those folks trustees. They ordered lots of sundries for the school and sometimes they find teachers to teach us for a few months here and there. But I did hear Ma say that Miss Bishop is going to stay another year as our teacher. I like that idea!

Pa says that sometimes the folks talk real loud at these meetings 'cause they want everybody to hear what they have to say. I guess they want everyone to know how they feel deep inside 'bout some things. Pa says they vote at their meetings. At the last meeting, the folks voted on getting some new desks and a 'grand set of maps' with the world on it. They're coming all the way from a place called Battle Creek in Michigan. Pa's thinking that those desks will be coming in by way of the Railway Depot in Galena. They say our school is going to become one of the finest around!

I heard Ma and Pa say that our rock school is different from the log or wood ones that folks usually build. I also remember Pa saying that Grandpa McDugal helped haul the limestone from the Galena hills. They used it for the walls of our school. Pa talks 'bout the men a long time ago crushing and boiling the limestone to make mortar. Then they set the rocks on top of each other. When they finished building the schoolhouse, the folks around here named the school after one of the first settlers in the Galena area. His name was Thomas Belden. His son is a grown man and he helps take care of the school by bringing us cords of wood or whatever our school needs. I've heard Pa call him Napoleon. Anyway, he probably feels proud-like since the school was named after his Pa.

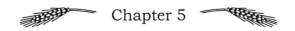

Chapter 5

NOT FEELING TOO GOOD

I don't always know what the big folks are talking 'bout, but I do know that me and Franky ain't getting along any better. The other day at recess time, I thought I'd go play by the creek with my pals. The creek always makes this gurgling sound like it's telling you to come and play. Sometimes I think I hear it say, "Come on and stay with me. Forget going back to school for the rest of the day." That creek makes it real hard for me not to listen to it, especially when it's nice outside. Anyway, me and the twins like going down there to see if there's any frogs we can catch. There's a big 'ol tree lying 'cross the creek, and we have fun jumping on the trunk and walking from one side to the other. But instead of catching frogs that day, Franky got all the boys to play a stickball game out in the field instead. He got to choose the kids he wanted on his team, like big Joey Walcher and Billy Kern, who's fast as lightning! I was the last one to be picked. The Kleck twins picked me, and so I went on their side.

Well, I was up to bat, and all my friends were watching. The girls were standing on the side watching, too. I swung, missed, and Franky laughed. I tried to hit the ball again and missed. Franky laughed even louder. When I missed it a third time, Franky got everyone to laugh. Then he ran up to me and shoved me down so hard, that my head was spinning.

Everyone was still laughing when I looked up and saw Miss Bishop watching me from the school door. She looked real sad. I just wanted to run to the creek, put my head in it and hide! Feeling like a darn fool, I got up instead and ran past Miss Bishop into school. I put my head down on the desk. I didn't know what else to do.

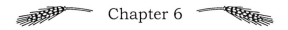 Chapter 6

THE CONTEST

Even though it's spring, I've got chores waiting for me every day, at home and at school. The first thing I do at school each morning is to open the shutters on the outside of the windows so the light can come in. Then I fetch water from the cold spring 'cross that creek that's always talking. All the children put their dippers in the bucket when they want a drink, so I know they're counting on me. At the end of the day, Miss Bishop cleans the slate board with the old drinking water from the bucket. I'm glad that it's getting warm and I don't have to get the firewood inside. That's one less chore to do.

Some days ago, I was on the way back to my seat from putting a full bucket of water down, when Franky tripped me walking by his desk. I went down, but no one saw. Darn! I've got to settle this with him once and for all, but I ain't real sure how to do it.

This morning, Miss Bishop asked if anyone wanted to help make new erasers. She's collected the things she needs to put them together. Mr. Studier gave her some sheepskin, and Miss Bishop already had tacks and small cut boards. I saw our old teacher, Mr. McHugh, make them once. He wrapped the sheepskin around the board and tacked it on. I was thinking that this could be fun, so I raised my hand, but Miss Bishop picked Maggie Brody instead.

Then Miss Bishop told us that a big store in the city—Sears, Roebuck and Company— is having a writing contest. They are asking school children to write an essay saying why they would want a flock of sheep of their very own. Miss Bishop says to think 'bout it long and hard and I am. Jeepers, who wouldn't want a flock of sheep? This contest might be real easy, and I can't wait to start writing!

I recall Pa saying that folks are trying to get more sheep on their farms in Galena. We've already got lots of cows, pigs, chickens and goats living here. I can't stop thinking 'bout this as I run up and down the hills on my way home. Huffing and puffing, I finally reach that 'ol creakin' back step and open the screen door. I grab a warm sugar cookie and a glass of milk, and then sit right down at the wooden supper table…still out of breath. Ma asks me to get right to my chores and I tell her I will real soon, but I have schoolwork to do first. She looks at me funny-like and shakes her head. I guess she's not used to me doing my schoolwork lickety-split. During planting and harvest season we don't have schoolwork 'cause we got work on the farm to do. And even when we do have schoolwork, I can't say that I hurry to get it done. Tonight's different though.

I find the backside of an old paper and start to write 'bout why I'd like—no, why I'd *love*—a flock of sheep. Well, just thinking 'bout it, makes the reasons fly out of my head and on to that paper! I can see it now. I'd be "King of the Hill" if I won that flock of sheep. The others would get out of my way when I herd my flock of sheep to Belden School. Maybe Miss Bishop would let them graze outside during the day, while I'm inside working on my lessons. Later, when my ewe has baby lambs, I'd give one to Miss Bishop and everyone in my class....except for Franky. Franky would be so red in the face when he saw that I was now "King of the Hill," that maybe he'd leave me alone.

Well, the first thing I do the next morning, is put my essay on Miss Bishop's desk. I must be grinning ear to ear, as Ma would say. I'm so excited! I think Miss Bishop is real excited for me, too. I'm wondering why, but

I'm too busy to think on it much. All I know is that I want that flock of sheep! Maggie Brody, the Kleck twins, big Joey Walcher and the rest of the class hand in their essays, too. Everybody except Franky. He never does his schoolwork!

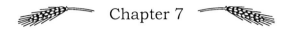 Chapter 7

SUMMER ON THE FARM

Summer is really here. The days are long, and it's so hot that we all play in the creek at recess. Miss Bishop comes out everyday and says not to. But, it's too late 'cause we're all dripping wet. It doesn't feel too good being damp the rest of the day while you're reading and writing. It doesn't smell too good either.

There's a new rope swing hanging from the branch of the old oak down by the creek. Franky's Pa put it there for the children to swing on at recess. I guess he felt he had to do something nice for the children at Belden School after Franky threw a ball and broke another glass window. Not really sure if he did it on purpose or not. You just never know with Franky. The new window cost his Pa 25 cents, and Franky had to help put it in on Saturday.

The crops are coming up real good now 'cause of the warm sun and spring rains. There ain't a lot of work to do in the fields, but cut the weeds down between the rows of corn, beans and peas. I help Ma in her flower and vegetable garden. She grows herbs for cooking, and is the best cook from here to Galena. Leastwise, that's what Pa says. Ma bakes delicious breads and pies. Once, she entered her raisin pie in the country fair and won first place! Pa said he knew she would win. When it's this hot, Ma moves her cooking out to the summer kitchen.

I do my chores on our farm after school when it's not so hot. I roll up my sleeves and get going as fast as I can, all the time thinking 'bout that flock of sheep I'm going to win. I'm also thinking that some of the hay I'm making with Pa will help feed them over the winter. I can't wait to find out if I'm the winner of the essay contest. Miss Bishop says we will find out before our harvest.

Ma has me pick wild blueberries and huckleberries on the hill behind our farm. She uses them in her pies and pancakes and then cans the rest for those long winter days when I'm wishing I was down by the creek again. I eat almost as many as I pick, but I know if I bring back a full pail of berries, Ma will let me go fishing. Today, I grab my pole, and run over the hill and through the valley to the Kleck farm pasture. I'm hoping maybe the twins can go fishing with me at the pond. But their Pa says they have too many chores to do in the field, so I go fishing alone.

Heading over the hill down Long Hollow Road, I remember what Pa said 'bout this land. He said that long ago, this hill was the burial ground for the Fox and Sauk Indians that once lived on our land. I have a hard time seeing them living on our land and farming it or going to school like I do. But Pa said no, that's not the way it was. He said that the Indians hunted for food, picked berries, ate meat, and went fishing just like I do. But they didn't farm the land like we do today, though they did grow corn. Sometimes the Indians would burn the prairies to flush out the game. Miss Bishop told us once that fire gives the prairie new life. They had families with grandparents, Ma's and Pa's and brothers and sisters. They lived in wigwams or lodges. They didn't go to Belden School, but they were taught important things by their parents and elders. Indian children had chores, played games, and probably had friend problems like I do with Franky.

Pa also said that the Indians didn't own the land 'cause they believed that people can't own Mother Earth. That's the name they call the woods, prairies, fields and skies—Mother Earth. I like that name. Pa believes like the Indians do that we're here to use the land in a good way. If we are good to the land, then our children someday can use it and pass it on to their children. I guess no one really owns the land. I think I understand. Pa sure knows a lot!

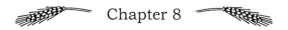

Chapter 8

HEADING INTO TOWN

I like going into Galena town with Pa especially in summer. We hitch up the horses and ride along Stagecoach Trail. From what folks around here say, Galena is famous 'cause of its lead mining. When we get into town, Pa visits with some men folk down by the Blacksmith Shop. He talks to them 'bout forging tools for the farm and some other things I don't rightly understand. Besides, I'm thinking 'bout more important things like maybe going to the general store for some candy. Pa always buys me a peppermint stick there. In hot weather, peppermint tastes mighty good. He might pick up some sugar and flour for Ma. Sometimes he surprises her with calico fabric and ribbon so she can make herself a new dress.

Before we leave town, Pa always takes me down to the Galena River so I can see the steamboats come in. The boats are mighty big, with paddlewheels behind them. The boats go back 'n forth down the river on their way to the Big Mississippi. Sometimes they unload lots of crates, and I wonder what's inside them. We watch as ladies and gentlemen in mighty fine clothes come down to the docks, waiting for their freight to be put on their wagons. Pretty horses and cows also come to Galena from far away on these boats, and I wonder if my sheep will come in here on boats like these.

The captains of these boats look mighty fancy, too, in their blue coats and hats with gold braid. Pa says that some of those captains live up in the hills behind Galena town. I look up into the hills from the dock and see big houses with lots of porches and a tiny room at the very top, almost like a church steeple. Pa laughs and says, "No, Peter, that's not a church steeple or even a room. It's a walkway so the family can see the boats coming up or down the river."

The big houses are made of red brick and stone, and some have those white wooden towers on top. I get dizzy looking up, and finally Pa says it's time to go. Horses and buggies, people calling to each other loudly, and dusty streets make Galena a busy place.

We head out of town towards our hill and down into our valley home where it is quiet. On the way, Pa talks 'bout General Grant. He says that he came to Galena on a steamboat to work at his Pa's tanning company and then left Galena to become a General in the Civil War. I guess Galena is proud 'cause it had twelve generals in that War. Some live here still. Anyway, Pa tells me that General Grant came back to town after the Civil War and the town just up and gave him a house on a hill! I guess the folks in Galena were mighty proud of him and wanted to show their appreciation. I heard Pa tell Ma that General Grant went on to become President of the United States. Imagine that!

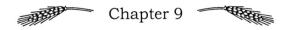

Chapter 9

The Winner

One day, it finally happens. Miss Bishop says she received a letter from the Sears, Roebuck and Company. She's planning on telling us after lunch who won the contest. I grab my dinner pail and go sit on an old hickory stump with the twins. I know that Ma has packed my favorite biscuits and gooseberry jam, but I don't pay much mind to what is in my pail. I'm too excited. We all talk 'bout what we will do with the flock if we win. I guess Miss Bishop made Franky do the essay anyway. He must have had something to say 'cause he told his pals that he would sell them at market and make lots of money.

I told him that the plan is to raise sheep on the farms in Galena. He said he doesn't care. He doesn't like sheep anyway.

I can't sit still waiting for the news after lunch. I run back to my desk and sit on my hands. It seems to take forever for Miss Bishop to open the big brown envelope and pull out that letter. She starts to talk 'bout how proud she is of everyone for writing an essay. Then she says she knows that everyone tried their best and really wanted to win. Miss Bishop hopes that we give the winner a pat on the back and say we're happy for them. I look over at Franky, and he has this "I don't care" grin on his face. I quickly look back at Miss Bishop 'cause she finally stopped talking.

I watch as her fingers slowly open the envelope. The day feels like it is moving as slow molasses and I can hardly wait. My heart is racing, and her words come out so slowly that every letter seems stretched out like a rattlesnake on a rock. Then she says, "The winner of the contest is...Peter McDugal!"

Everyone turns to look at me and stare. First, one person claps, then another claps, and another, until everyone in the room is clapping for me...except Franky. It hits me like a lightning bolt. I won!

Miss Bishop is so excited for me. I kind of wonder why, but then I figure it out. I remember thinking that Miss Bishop always likes to make things better for the children of her school. Well, I think she is happy for me 'cause I'm feeling better 'bout myself. I know I won fair and square. But Miss Bishop knew all along that if I really wanted a flock of sheep, I'd write one good essay.

Now, if I could only fix up what's broke between me and Franky. Well, I'll work on that later. Right now, I'm looking forward to having my own flock of sheep. I'm going have a lot of work to do, but I've got time now that school will be out for a spell. What with helping Ma and Pa with the harvest and working with my sheep, I'm going be the happiest boy alive!

What seems like a month of Sundays later, my ewe, ram, and a few young sheep are special delivered in a big wagon by a city-looking man. Pa greets him down by the farm gate. The man says, "I'm looking for Peter McDugal. I've got a special delivery from the Sears, Roebuck and Company, and it's *hungry*!"

The sheep are all real pretty and fluffy white, especially the ram.He has a black face and looks like he is the master of the flock. The Kleck twins come over right away to see my special delivery flock. The other kids stop by after they are done with their harvesting chores. Even Miss Bishop comes to visit. But, not Franky.

My flock takes a lot of hard work, and Pa helps me when he is able. I've got to feed them, clean their pens, wash their wool, shear them, and put them out to graze. I also have to keep watch for coyotes. Coyote like to kill

sheep and that scares me, so I stay with them all the time. But I'm not sure what I'm going to do when school starts again.

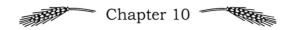

Chapter 10

A Surprise in the Field

"I can tell fall is coming," Ma says one day. I think she's right. The hills are turning a yellowish-orange color. The nights are cooler. And Pa is putting in his bid to do work at Belden School. There was a special school meeting called the other night. Those trustee folks were asking for someone to whitewash the school, clean inside, and clean the chimney and stove pipe for the winter. Pa asked for less money than the others, so he got the job. Maggie Brody's Pa is putting on new shingles since some of them blew off in a storm last spring. Mr. Kleck got the job for putting together the new school desks. I think Pa's going to help him 'cause he's got to haul them all the way from the Railway Depot in Galena. I'm thinking that I'm mighty proud to go to school at Belden. It seems that all the families that are part of our Belden community help to pull together to make it the finest rock schoolhouse in this tiny corner of Illinois. I know where we live 'cause we looked at it on the big map in school!

Yesterday, I was walking over the hill to the Berloff Farm to help old Mr. Berloff with his cows. He fell and hurt his arm, so I've been milking his cows. I hated to leave my flock since I'm "King of the Hill" now, but Ma and Pa said I had to go. As I was crossing the creek and coming around the old oak, some turkeys came at me from the other side. They scared me out of my wits, squawking the way they do. But then I got to day dreaming 'bout how good they're going taste at Thanksgiving time, with Ma's cranberry sauce and Grandma's McDugal's sausage stuffing! I can't wait 'till Pa brings one of them home. My mouth is watering already.

Well, as I was coming out into the field, the grasshoppers started popping up everywhere and jumping in my hair. Then, I heard the hum of the locust and something else...a crying-like noise. I'm searching and looking all around the wheat field. Finally, I saw the top of somebody's head sticking out of the prairie grass and rocking back and forth. I got a little closer and looked down at a face that was all scrunched up in pain. It was Franky's face. He was holding his foot, and crying and whimpering like a baby. His face was so scrunched up that his eyes were shut tight. But when he took a breath so he could start crying again, he looked up and saw me standing over him. I can tell you that he was pretty darn surprised to see me!

"Franky, why are you carrying on and crying like that?" I asked, but he just cried louder.

Then with his next big breath, he yelled out, "I twisted my darn ankle in one of those ground hog holes. It hurts, Peter, real bad!"

He was bawling like a baby thinking nobody would find him before dark. I guess he was just plain scared. I guess he wasn't thinking I'd be the one that would come along and find him laying out here.

"Franky, I was on my way to help old Mr. Berloff with his cows. Stay put, and I'll run over to Belden School. Maybe my Pa is there doing some work. Don't worry. I'll help 'ya Franky!" I wanted to let him know that I would help him, but that I was his friend, too. Ma and Pa always told me to help folks when their in trouble or crying in a field I guess like Franky.

"I'll be here, but hurry. It hurts somethin' terrible," Franky said while he was making those crying-like noises in his throat again. I don't understand it. Franky is always so tough and bossy, and now he can't even catch a breath 'cause he's crying so much.

I ran as fast as I could over the hill, until I saw Belden School in the valley. It sure was a welcome sight. Pa and some of the neighbors were doing their work. It looked like our school

was getting a new set of clothes. Mr. Brody was putting on the shingles. Mr. Schown was inside cleaning. Mr. Kleck was stacking cords of wood and Pa was cleaning the stovepipe. I wanted to stand there and watch everyone do their share, but I had to hurry. I told Pa what happened. Pa and Mr. Brody got the wagon, and we headed back lickety-split over the hill to where Franky was still sitting in the grasses, rocking back and forth, holding his foot, and making those crying-like noises.

The men picked up Franky and put him on top of some old blankets to soften the bumpy wagon ride. When we got to Franky's farm, his Ma and Pa were there to take him inside. He sure did get scolded 'cause he was supposed to help his Pa harvest their north field, but he ran off instead. They still hugged him, though, and fixed him right up. Franky's one lucky boy to have folks like that.

Chapter 11

An Understanding

Today, I'm out with my flock and guess who comes hobbling over the hill? Yep! Franky. It turns out that his foot ain't as bad as he thought. But it is still sore, he says. I'm thinking he was more scared of not being found until morning and laying there in the dark listening to the night noises.

"My Ma and Pa told me to come over and say thanks for finding me yesterday. 'Ya know, I was ready to get up and walk back home, but when I saw you coming, I thought I might as well just lie there, take it easy like and wait for a wagon ride. But thanks, Peter, just the same."

Now, I know he's telling a big fib, 'cause he was sure hurting yesterday, and I saw him crying something awful. But I guess he felt he had to say that so he'd feel better. And that's all right with me. I know he's not as tough as our pals think, and he knows that I know the real story. It's like we have a secret now tying us together like rope. We don't have to say anything or fight it out, but we both know the truth.

Well, for the rest of our harvest time, Franky has been coming over to help me with my small flock when he ain't working with his Pa. Come spring, my ewe will be having some baby lambs and then there's shearing time. I'm real excited and so is Franky. He asked if he could have a lamb next spring and I said, "Sure".

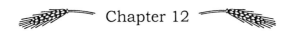

Chapter 12

Friends

Fall is here and we are all together again at Belden School. The schoolhouse looks real happy to see me and my friends. It always seems to come to life when we're playing outside, or we're sitting inside its walls working on our lessons. I'm real glad to see my friends again, too, including Franky.

Miss Bishop is standing at the door greeting all of us. I know that she's coming to stay at our farm for the fall. But I don't care 'cause I'm real glad she's teaching at Belden School again this year. She's got a big smile on her face when me and Franky walk past her talking 'bout my flock.

Boy, oh boy, Belden School looks real nice inside and out! Our Pa's did a good job. The school is whitewashed and the new desks are waiting inside for us. The newly shingled roof will keep us dry in spring. I can see that the cords of wood are stacked on the side of Belden, waiting for me to bring it inside during the cold winter. I put my dinner pail inside the freshly whitewashed cloakroom, come out, and walk across the creaky wood floor to my new desk in the back of the room. It smells clean inside like soap on a Saturday night. The big flag hangs on the wall proud-like. The slate board says "Welcome Back" and the new erasers are sitting on the ledge.

Just as I'm looking round at all the new things that have been done to Belden School, I hear Miss Bishop say, "Peter, don't forget to fetch the water from the spring, and stack the firewood please. Franky, could you help Peter with the school chores this year?" Franky nods his head and smiles. Yep! It's good to be back at Belden School again!

THE STORY BEHIND THE STORY

Belden School in still very much alive in the hills of Galena. It was lost to the woods that grew up around it and kept it out of sight for others to see. A few years ago, I was asked to research its history and try to revive our hidden treasure. Belden School was sitting quietly for me to discover. As a teacher of Social Studies, I couldn't wait to begin my journey. I started by interviewing local neighbors who were once students at Belden School many years ago. Next, I poured through numerous books about Galena and its history. A local historian also told tales of long ago and presented two old journals of Belden School that he had saved. In those journals, were records of all the meetings, elections and purchases dating back to the year of 1873.

I dedicate this fictional story to Belden School, in hope that the stories of those who lived their life within its walls remain alive. I also respectfully acknowledge Mr. Bob Kleckner. His lively stories and guidance brought this book to life. I also want to acknowledge the work of the present Belden School Committee, which has the daunting task of raising funds for its restoration, and convincing all who will listen how important it is to keep our history alive so that our children will learn and understand where they've come from and where they need go in the future. May we preserve and protect our heritage always.

p.j. hartenaus
August 2007

Belden School in the hills of the Galena Territory long ago

Belden School students in the early 1900s

Students inside the rock schoolhouse

Students of all ages at the Belden School

Account of Current Expenditures.

The account of Expenditures should be audited on the first day of each successive month, or at least as often as on the first day of each succeeding three months, and the amount paid by the Treasurer. The payment should be properly acknowledged at the bottom of the account.

DATE.			DESCRIPTION OF ITEMS OF EXPENDITURES.	AMOUNT.	
Month.	Day.	Year.		Dollars.	Cts.
June	5	1886	for Crayon	—	25
"	"	"	" Sundries for School.	—	50
"	"	"	to pay for School Desks, to Union School Furniture Co. Battle Creek, Mich.	90	00
"	"	"	To James H. Sale for hauling and puting up School Desks.	5	00
"	"	"	" Wm. A. Studier for hauling and puting up School Desks.	5	00
June	10	"	" Teresa E. Krengel for teaching 1 M.	20	00
July	1	"	" " " " from June 9 till June 30.	15	00
Sept.	11	"	To Teresa E. Krengel for teaching from July 1. to September the 8. 28 days	25	00
October	2	"	To Wm. A. Studier to pay for two rear seats	7	00
"	"	"	Daily Register.	1	00
"	"	"	Crayon.	—	25
"	"	"	for Sundries for School.	—	30
"	22	"	For six cord of good drey oak wood at $ 2. 80 per cord. to Mr. Erin	16	80
Novemb.	11	"	Mr. T. Mc Donald for sawing six cord of wood at 75c. per cord.	4	50
"	13	"	To pai freight on School Maps.	—	75
"	"	"	Getting Slot fixt.	—	30
"	"	"	Crayon.	—	25
"	"	"	Sending Order to Thomas Co. Chicago.	—	5
"	"	"	One Window glass	—	10

Old ledger sheet from the 1880s of items purchased for the school

Record of Special Election.
(State of Illinois.)
Guilford March 27, 1886.

The legally qualified voters residing in District No. Five in Town ship No. 28 N. Range No. Two East in Jo Daviess County, and State of Illinois, pursuant to notices given as required by law, held their Special Election at the School House in said District on Saturday the 27 day of March 1886, for the purpose of elec ting for this said District one Director to fill the unexpired term of John Schuk whose office expired at the Annual District Election 1887 occasioned by his removal from said District.

J. Henry Sale,
Conrad Balbach,   acted as Judges,
William A. Studier, as Clerk of the election. The polls were opened at 4 o'clock P. M., and closed at 6 o'clock P. M., according to the notices given as above stated.

James Sheridan having received a majority of votes cast for the unexpired term, was declared duly elected School Director of the said District for one year and one month, to fill the unexpired term of John Schuk whose office expired at the Annual District Election 1887 as above stated.

J. H. Sale
Conrad Balbach
Judges.
William A. Studier. Clerk.

Record of a special election at
Belden back in the 1880s

Time passes on and Belden School is overcome by the surrounding woods.

Belden School as of 2007.
The restoration process is in progress.

CPSIA information can be obtained at www.ICGtesting.com
Printed in the USA
LVOW080509190313

324840LV00001B/7/P

9 781434 383518